by
ISABEL OTTER

Illustrated by
HARRIET LYNAS

This
LOVE

tiger tales

It doesn't matter who we are—
join hands and stand up tall.
Love is a special language
that's understood by all.

Graceful birds swoop low and dive,

soaring through the air.

We watch in quiet wonder,

a moment of joy to share.

We nestle close together in our cozy little nook,

the words
painting pictures

as we share
our favorite book.

We roam the streets as one,

Dog always at my side.

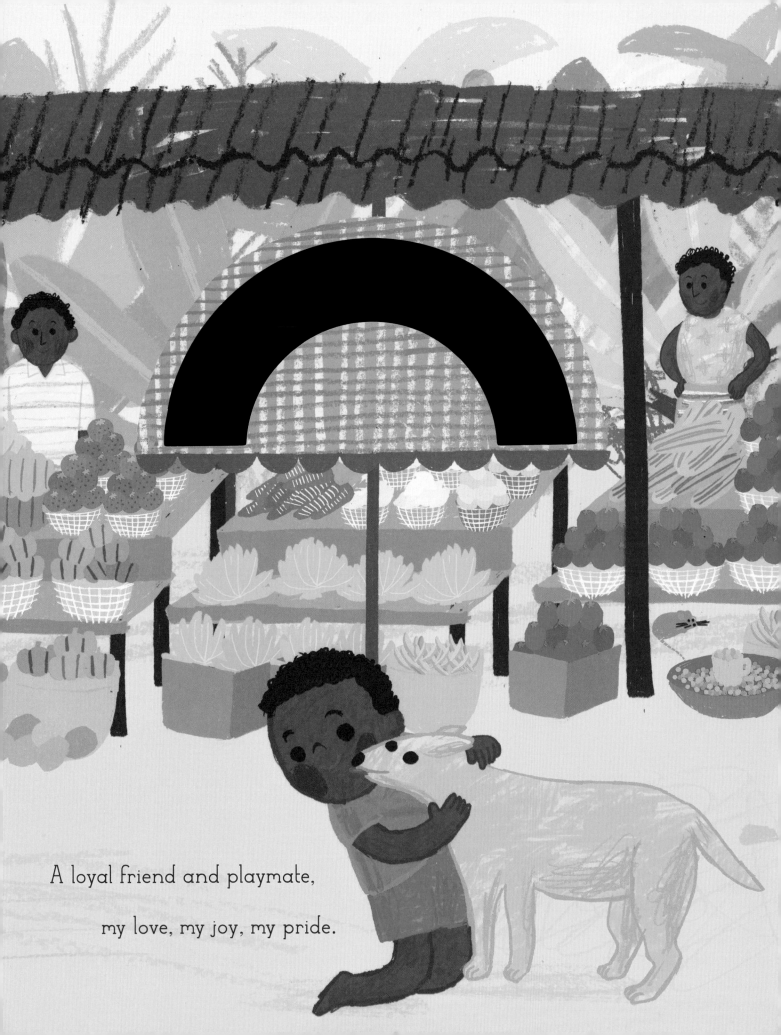

A loyal friend and playmate,

my love, my joy, my pride.

We laugh and play all day

under stormy skies.

Splish, splash! We love the rain.

What a great surprise.

I watch the crystal carpet form

as balls of snow are flung.

Soft flakes float gently on the air,

then melt on my warm tongue.

Colored streamers burst and pop,

lighting up the night.

Goodnight kisses for us all

as sparks fade from sight.

We dig a hole, then scatter seeds
to take care of our land.

My grandpa teaches me to sow
with patient, loving hands.

We'll dance and prance in fountains, make rainbows in the spray.

We love to leap and twirl around—please, can we stay all day?

Can you hear a drip, drip, drop?

Rain is falling fast!

And though the seasons come and go, our special bond will last.

Dad's safe hands are guiding me, and now I'm on my own!

I know he's right behind me; I'll never feel alone.

We share our laughter, songs, and tales
while parrots preen and call.

The sun is winking on the sea
as dusk begins to fall.

My baby brother has been born;
I must take care of him.
His tiny finger curls around mine;
my heart fills to the brim.

It doesn't matter who we are—
join hands and stand up tall.
Love is a special language
that's understood by all.